COUNTRIES IN THE NEWS

# THE UNITED KINGDOM

## Kieran Walsh

Rourke

Publishing LLC

Vero Beach, Florida 32964

www.rourkepublishing.com

The country's flag is correct at the time of going to press.

PHOTO CREDITS: ©Ian Britton Cover, pg 16, 17; ©UK Press/Getty pg 13; ©Adam Pretty/Getty pg 15; ©Craig Young pg 18; ©Jane Haselden pg 6; ©Simaon Cataudo pg 11; ©David Hewitt pg 7; All other images © Peter Langer Associated Media Group

Title page: *A Londoner feeds pigeons in Trafalgar Square.*

Editor: Frank Sloan

Cover and interior design by Nicola Stratford

**Library of Congress Cataloging-in-Publication Data**

Walsh, Kieran.
  The United Kingdom / Kieran Walsh.
    p. cm. --  (Countries in the news)
  Includes bibliographical references and index.
  ISBN 1-59515-174-5 (hardcover)
  1.  Great Britain--Juvenile literature. 2.  Northern Ireland--Juvenile literature.  I. Title.  II.
Series: Walsh, Kieran. Countries in the news.
  DA27.5.W35 2004
  941--dc22
                              2004009684

Printed in the USA

CG/CG

# TABLE OF CONTENTS

# WELCOME TO THE UNITED KINGDOM

The United Kingdom (UK) is made up of a group of islands off the coast of northwestern Europe. The country is just north of France and Spain and west of Belgium, the Netherlands, and Germany.

*The gates in front of Buckingham Palace, where Queen Elizabeth II lives*

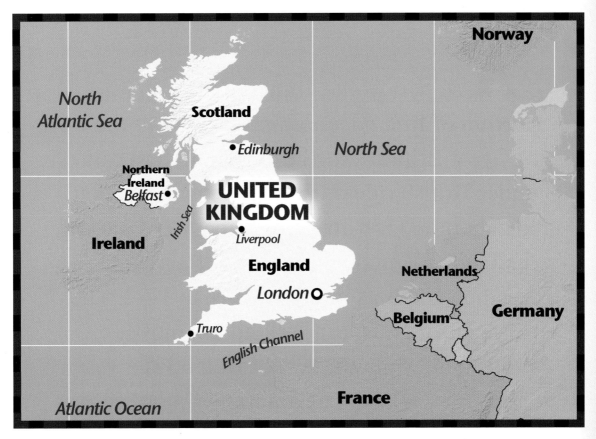

The largest island is Great Britain, which is divided into England to the south, Wales to the west, and Scotland to the north. The largest portion of the population lives in England. Much smaller islands like the Isle of Wight, the Isle of Man, and the Orkney Islands surround Great Britain.

The islands of the United Kingdom together cover an area roughly twice the size of New York State.

**A**lso part of the United Kingdom is a **portion** of Ireland, an island located to the west of Great Britain. Northern Ireland first came under British rule during the reign of Queen Elizabeth I (1558-1603). It remained a part of the United Kingdom even after the rest of Ireland gained its **independence** in 1922. The residents of Northern Ireland are mostly Protestant, while the rest of Ireland is generally Catholic.

London is one of the world's great cities. Other major cities in Great Britain include Manchester, Birmingham, and Liverpool. Edinburgh and Glasgow are large cities in Scotland.

*Edinburgh Castle, a well-known site in Edinburgh, Scotland*

*Surf lashes the coast of Northern Ireland.*

Northern Ireland is one of the last remaining parts of the British Empire, which once included India, Australia, parts of Africa, and the original 13 colonies of America.

# THE PEOPLE

The United Kingdom has a large population, but the quality of life there is very good. The life expectancy in the UK is 77 years.

Clothing, family life, and housing are very much the same as in the United States. Although it is spoken with an **accent**, English is the country's official language. Some people, though, also speak Welsh, Scottish Gaelic, and Irish Gaelic.

*Crowds gather on a sunny day in London's Leicester Square.*

**The entrance to one of London's Underground (subway) stations**

The United Kingdom is one of the most **technologically** advanced countries in the world. Most people in the UK own or have access to televisions, phones, and computers.

The United Kingdom is home to **immigrants** from all over the world. There are large numbers of people from India, Pakistan, and Bangladesh. People also migrate to the UK from China, Russia, Poland, Italy, Spain, and Africa.

About 45 percent of the population of the United Kingdom are members of the Anglican Church. Another 15 percent are Roman Catholic. There are smaller numbers of Muslims, Presbyterians, and Methodists.

*"Big Ben," the nickname for one of the world's most famous sights*

*The ruins of Hadrian's Wall in the north of England*

*The ancient stones of Stonehenge dot the southern English countryside.*

# LIFE IN THE UNITED KINGDOM

**D**ifferences between life in the United States and in the United Kingdom are **subtle**. In America, people drive cars on the right-hand side of the road. In Britain, they drive on the left. Familiar things often have different names, such as lorry (truck), trainers (sneakers), and crisps (potato chips).

Many **institutions** in the United Kingdom are owned and controlled by the government.

*A car proceeds toward Buckingham Palace, on the left side of the road!*

Queen Elizabeth II visits with two students in Windsor, England.

The British Broadcasting Corporation (BBC), for instance, is state-run. Likewise, the National Health Service, which most people in Britain depend on for their health care, is a government body.

# SCHOOL AND SPORTS

The United Kingdom has an outstanding educational system. Most British children attend primary school from the ages of 5 to 11 and usually continue to secondary school until at least the age of 16. After secondary school, students often take exams for placement at one of the UK's many **esteemed** universities. The most popular sport in the UK is football, but it is not the version of football with which you are familiar. Football in the UK is what you probably know as soccer.

*Keeping cool in the fountain in London's Trafalgar Square.*

*A shot of the England vs. Australia rugby World Cup final*

Another extremely popular sport in Britain is rugby. In fact, since England won the rugby World Cup in 2003 over Australia, it is possible that rugby is now even more popular in the UK than football.

The **literacy** rate in the UK is 99 percent.

# FOOD AND HOLIDAYS

Traditional British food includes items such as steak-and-kidney pie, scones with butter and jam, fish and chips (French fries), and the national drink, tea. However, the arrival of immigrants from around the world into Britain has also made room for dishes like curries, sushi, and a variety of vegetarian cooking.

Probably no holiday is more important to the English than Christmas. Some English Christmas traditions are crackers (cardboard tubes filled with small gifts), mince pies and Christmas pudding, and the **annual** television address given by the Queen.

*A scene of the Welsh countryside*

*Christmas celebrations take place at an ice rink in Edinburgh, Scotland.*

Other holidays celebrated in the UK include Bonfire Night, Bank Holidays, and Boxing Day—the day after Christmas!

*An old English tradition: the Royal Guards parade on horseback.*

*The harbor of Girvan, on the west coast of Scotland*

# THE FUTURE

**I**n recent times, the United Kingdom has successfully dealt with a number of major problems, including the spread of mad cow disease, an unstable economy, and **terrorism**.

The United States started as a colony of Great Britain. Our lifestyles are similar and we even speak the same language. Naturally, we feel a greater kinship with the United Kingdom than with most other countries of the world.

The United States has had differences with the United Kingdom in the past. Despite this, Great Britain remains one of our closest allies. There is no doubt that our futures are strongly connected.

# FAST FACTS

**Area:** 94,525 square miles  (244,801 sq km)

**Borders:** Atlantic Ocean, North Sea, Irish Sea, Celtic Sea, English Channel, and portions of Ireland

**Population:** 60,094,648
**Monetary Unit:**  Pound Sterling

**Largest Cities:**  London, Glasgow, Birmingham, Liverpool, Edinburgh
**Government:**  Constitutional Monarchy

**Religions:**  Anglican, Roman Catholic, Muslim, Presbyterian, Methodist
**Crops:**  Cereals, oilseed, potatoes, vegetables

**Natural Resources:**  Coal, petroleum, natural gas, tin, limestone, iron ore, salt, clay, chalk, gypsum, lead
**Major Industries:**  Machine tools, electric power equipment, railroad equipment, shipbuilding, aircraft, motor vehicles and parts, electronics and communications equipment, metals, chemicals, coal, petroleum, paper and paper products, food processing, textiles

# THE BRITISH GOVERNMENT

The United Kingdom does not have a president. Instead, it has a Prime Minister and a monarchy. The Prime Minister is elected, while Elizabeth II will remain Queen for as long as she wishes. Currently, the Prime Minister of Britain is Tony Blair.

If the Prime Minister is like the president, **Parliament** is a bit like the American Congress. Like Congress, Parliament is where laws are passed. Parliament also controls government use of money.

*London's Tower Bridge crosses the River Thames.*

# GLOSSARY

**accent** (AK sent) — a distinctive manner of speech

**annual** (ANN yoo uhl) — yearly

**esteemed** (es TEEMD) — well regarded

**immigrants** (IM uh grantz) — people who move from one country to another

**independence** (IN deh PEN dents) — freedom; self-rule

**institutions** (IN steh TOO shunz) — organizations

**literacy** (LIT eh ruh see) — the ability to read and write

**Parliament** (PAR luh ment) — the legislative body of the United Kingdom

**portion** (POR shun) — a part of something; a piece

**subtle** (SUH til) — quiet, not overbearing

**technologically** (TEK no laj uk lee) — relating to the use of science and machines to make life easier

**terrorism** (TER er iz um) — the use of violence to threaten people

# FURTHER READING

Find out more about The United Kingdom with these helpful books:

- Bramwell, Martyn: *The World in Maps: Europe*. Lerner Publications, 2000.
- Campbell, Kumari. *Visual Geography: The United Kingdom in Pictures.* Lerner Publications, 2004.
- Deady, Kathleen W. *Countries of the World: England.* Bridgestone Books, 2001.
- Faiella, Graham. *England: A Primary Source Cultural Guide.* Rosen Publishing Group, 2004.
- Heinrichs, Ann. *Enchantment of the World: Wales*. Children's Press, 2003.
- Hull, Lisa. *Countries of the World: Scotland.* Gareth Stevens, 2003.

# WEBSITE TO VISIT

- www.infoplease.com/ipa/A0108078.html
  Infoplease.com – United Kingdom

# INDEX

## About the Author

Kieran Walsh is a writer of children's nonfiction books, primarily on historical and social studies topics. Walsh has been involved in the children's book field as editor, proofreader, and illustrator as well as author.